Hayley Wickenheiser

by Chelsea Donaldson

Gail Saunders-Smith, PhD, Consulting Editor

CAPSTONE PRESS

a capstone imprint

Pebble Plus is published by Capstone Press,
1710 Roe Crest Drive, North Mankato, Minnesota 56003
www.capstonepub.com

Cataloging-in-publication data is on file with the Library of Congress
ISBN 978-1-4914-1958-8 (library binding)
ISBN 978-1-4914-1977-9 (paperback)
ISBN 978-1-4914-1990-8 (ebook PDF)
Written by Chelsea Donaldson

Developed and Produced by Focus Strategic Communications, Inc.
Adrianna Edwards: project manager
Ron Edwards: editor
Rob Scanlan: designer and compositor
Mary Rose MacLachlan: media researcher

Photo Credits
AP Images: Lehtikuva, Jussi Nukari, 17; Calgary Herald, 21; Canadian Press Images: Sean Kilpatrick, Title Page, Larry MacDougal, 5, Ryan Remiorz, 9, Hans Deryk, 11; Landov: Reuters/ Herb Swanson, cover; Newscom: Phillippe Millereau / DPPI / Icon SMI, 13, Adrian Dennis / AFP, 15, Mike Blake / Reuters, 19; Shutterstock: Foto011, 7.

Note to Parents and Teachers
The Canadian Biographies set supports national curriculum standards for social studies related to people and culture. This book describes and illustrates Hayley Wickenheiser. The images support early readers in understanding text. The repetition of words and phrases helps early readers learn new words. This book also introduces early readers to subject-specific vocabulary words, which are defined in the Glossary section. Early readers may need assistance to read some words and to use the Table of Contents, Glossary, Read More, Internet Sites, and Index sections of the book.

Printed in China by Leo Paper Group in 2014
007039LEOF14

Table of Contents

Early Years

Hayley Wickenheiser is

a star Canadian hockey player.

She was born in 1978,

in Shaunavon, Saskatchewan.

Hayley played hockey

as soon as she could walk!

born in
Shaunavon,
Saskatchewan

1978

Shaunavon, Saskatchewan

Hayley's family moved to Calgary

when she was 13 years old.

By then Hayley was a star

on the girls' hockey team.

Soon she started playing

on a boys' team.

born in
Shaunavon,
Saskatchewan

1978   1991

moves to
Calgary

6

Hayley played on a boys' hockey team like this one.

Young Adult

At age 15 Hayley joined the

Canadian women's hockey team.

Her first big series was the

World Championship in 1994.

Hayley and her team beat the

U.S. team in the championship.

Hayley (top row, fourth from left) and the Canadian women's hockey team at the 1994 World Championship

Hayley played in the first women's Olympic hockey game in 1998. Hayley and the Canadian team won silver medals. But they were not happy. Next time they wanted to win gold!

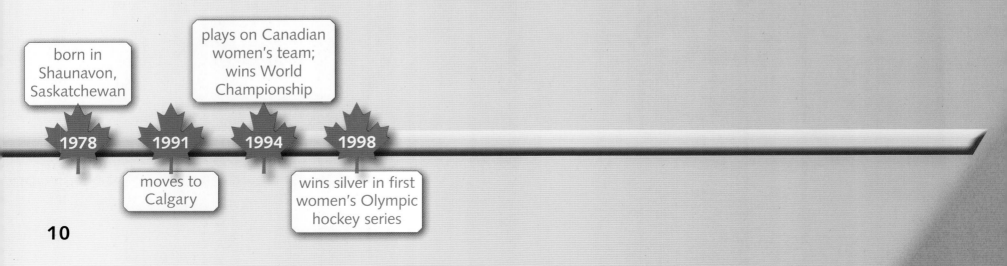

born in Shaunavon, Saskatchewan

plays on Canadian women's team; wins World Championship

1978   1991   1994   1998

moves to Calgary

wins silver in first women's Olympic hockey series

The Canadian women's hockey team at the 1998 Olympic Games

Hayley was busy on the ice.
But life off the ice was
important too. In 2001
Hayley adopted a boy named
Noah. Hayley says Noah is
the best person in her life.

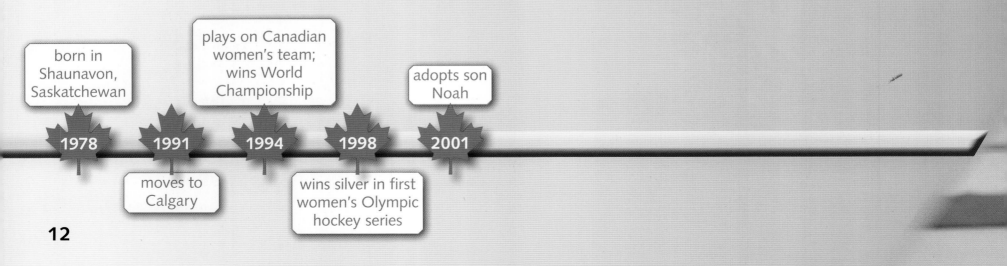

born in
Shaunavon,
Saskatchewan

plays on Canadian
women's team;
wins World
Championship

adopts son
Noah

1978   1991   1994   1998   2001

moves to
Calgary

wins silver in first
women's Olympic
hockey series

Hayley with her son Noah at the 2002 Olympics

Becoming the Best

In 2002 the Canadian team got another chance at an Olympic gold medal. This time they beat their American rivals 3–2. Hayley was voted Most Valuable Player.

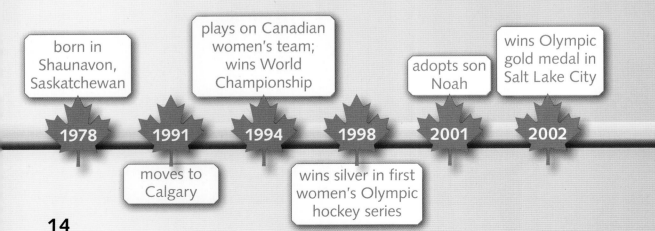

born in Shaunavon, Saskatchewan		plays on Canadian women's team; wins World Championship		adopts son Noah	wins Olympic gold medal in Salt Lake City
1978	**1991**	**1994**	**1998**	**2001**	**2002**
	moves to Calgary		wins silver in first women's Olympic hockey series		

Hayley scored a goal in an Olympic game in 2002.

Hayley was the best female player in the world. But she needed a new challenge. She moved to Finland to play on a men's hockey team. Hayley soon became a superstar there.

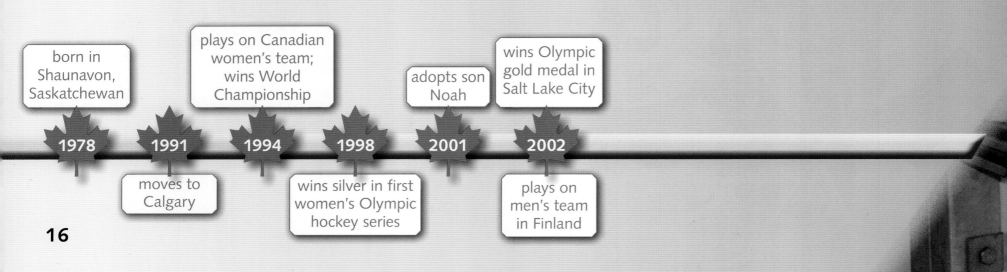

born in Shaunavon, Saskatchewan

plays on Canadian women's team; wins World Championship

adopts son Noah

wins Olympic gold medal in Salt Lake City

1978   1991   1994   1998   2001   2002

moves to Calgary

wins silver in first women's Olympic hockey series

plays on men's team in Finland

Hayley with some teammates in Finland

Hayley has played hockey for Canada in every Olympic Games since 1998. They have won one silver and four gold medals. They have also won eight World Championship games.

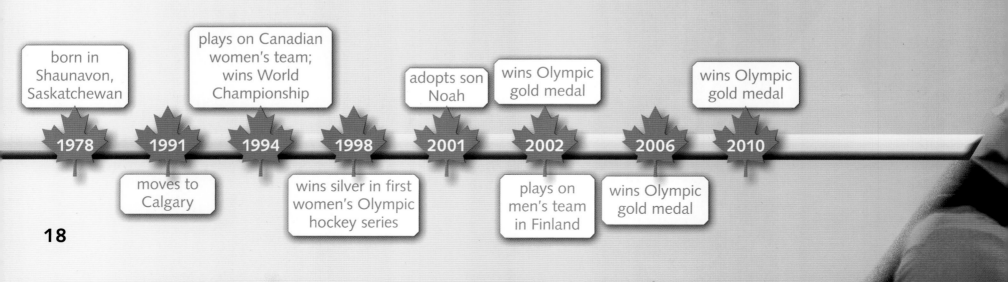

born in Shaunavon, Saskatchewan

plays on Canadian women's team; wins World Championship

adopts son Noah

wins Olympic gold medal

wins Olympic gold medal

| 1978 | 1991 | 1994 | 1998 | 2001 | 2002 | 2006 | 2010 |

moves to Calgary

wins silver in first women's Olympic hockey series

plays on men's team in Finland

wins Olympic gold medal

Hayley (center) with her son and teammates

Hayley Today

In 2013 Hayley graduated from the University of Calgary. The next year Hayley and the Canadian team won another Olympic gold medal. Hayley is a star both on and off the ice.

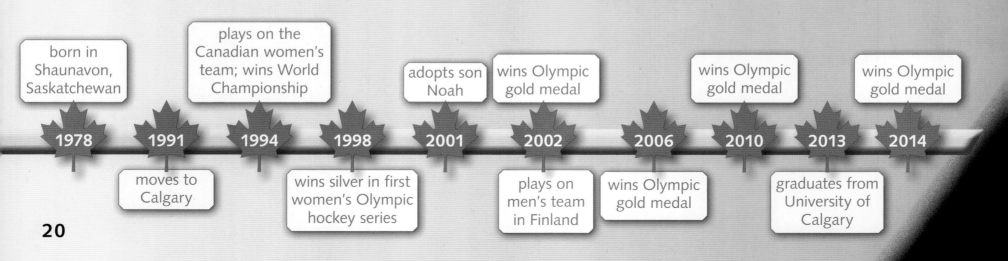

born in Shaunavon, Saskatchewan

plays on the Canadian women's team; wins World Championship

adopts son Noah

wins Olympic gold medal

wins Olympic gold medal

wins Olympic gold medal

1978   1991   1994   1998   2001   2002   2006   2010   2013   2014

moves to Calgary

wins silver in first women's Olympic hockey series

plays on men's team in Finland

wins Olympic gold medal

graduates from University of Calgary

Hayley at her university graduation

Glossary

adopt—to make a child a legal member of a family

rival—someone with whom you compete

series—a set of games

Read More

Durrie, Karen. *Hockey*. Calgary: Weigl, 2012.

MacGregor, Roy, and **Geneviève Després**. *The Highest Number in the World*. Toronto: Tundra Books, 2014.

Internet Sites

FactHound offers a safe, fun way to find Internet sites related to this book. All of the sites on FactHound have been researched by our staff.

Here's all you do:

Visit *www.facthound.com*

Type in this code: 9781491419588

Check out projects, games and lots more at
www.capstonekids.com

Index

Word Count: 269
Grade: 1
Early-Intervention Level: 16